KU-560-596

This book belongs to:

_____

_____

_____

For Sonny.

Published by **KAMA** Publishing

19A The Swale, Norwich, NR5 9HE

www.kamapublishing.co.uk

Text © Kevin Price, 2014
Illustrations © Vicky Fieldhouse, 2014

All rights reserved. No part may be reproduced, stored in a retrieval
system, or transmitted in any form or by any means, electronic,
mechanical, photocopying or otherwise without the prior
permission in writing of the author.

British Library Cataloguing in Publishing Data.
A catalogue record for this book is available from the British Library.

ISBN 978-0-9567196-6-9

Printed in the European Union by Druk-Intro s.a.

FEEDING TIME AT THE ZOO

Kevin Price   Vicky Fieldhouse

It's animal feeding time down at the Zoo.
Bertie is there and he's brought Maisie too.

Today she is having a wonderful treat;
She's learning about what the animals eat.
She's taking the food cart around by herself,
To find out what they eat to stay in good health.

Maisie sets off, where's she going to first?
She's off to the Lion's den, fearing the worst!

But what should she give him? Are vegetables best?
She throws him a cabbage – he isn't impressed!

He roars, "You should know that my meal's not complete,
Until you have thrown me a big piece of meat!"

She's down at the forest, the monkeys are there.
They pull funny faces and ruffle her hair.
She wonders aloud, "What do they like to eat?
Are they like the Lion? Do they want some meat?"

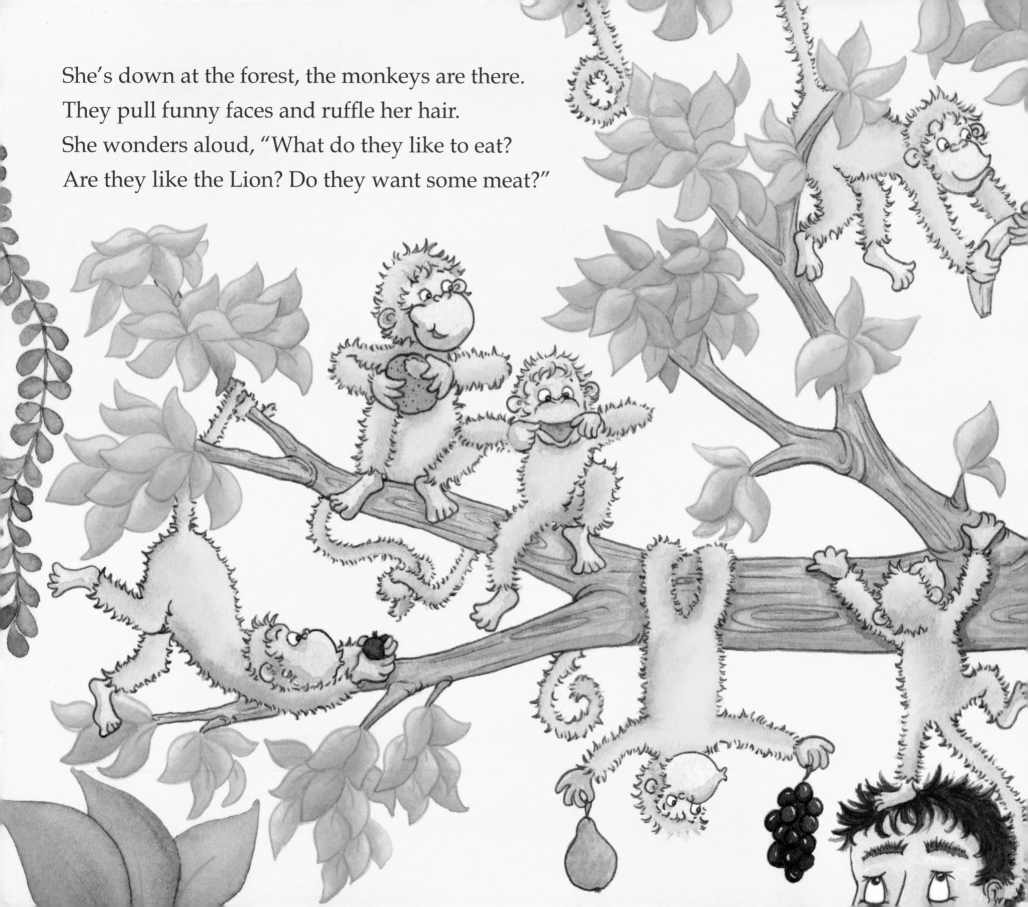

The monkeys all giggle, they think it's a hoot!
"Oh Maisie, you're silly, we'd just like some fruit!"

The bird cages next, Maisie's there with the Parrot.
She asks if he might like an onion or carrot.
He squawks, "I will tell you what this parrot needs;
A bowlful of fruit or a handful of seeds!"
He turns his head sideways and lets out a screech,
"I fancy some fruit! Could you find me a peach?"

She's there with the Elephant, what does he scoff?
A kiwi fruit, melon and pineapple broth?
The Elephant says, "While a little might suit,
An elephant cannot survive on just fruit.
Although I'll eat leaves if you find me a hedge,
What I need is lashings and lashings of veg!"

Maisie has made her way down to the pool.
She's paddling her feet in and keeping them cool.

The penguins are giving their tummies a rub.
They shout, "Come on Maisie! Please give us our grub!
We hope you've prepared us our favourite dish -
A bucket of stinky and succulent fish!"

She's there with the meerkats – oh, aren't they so cute!
She offers them vegetables, red meat and fruit.

The eldest one says, as he stands on hind legs,
"We might prefer meal worms, or little birds' eggs!
We're partial to crickets and fat, slimy slugs
And all sorts of other delectable bugs!"

Panda is next, what does she like to eat?

Perhaps she likes vegetables, insects or meat?

"Not me," says the Panda, "those things are all yuck!
But I have to tell you that you are in luck.
I'm easy to please - I'm the best in the Zoo,
All I need to eat is a piece of bamboo."

Maisie is standing alongside the Camel,
Who sometimes is quite the most bad-tempered mammal!
He says, "Hurry up! Come on, give me some hay!
And get me a drink before you go away!
You really should know, as the zookeeper's daughter,
When camels get thirsty we need lots of water!"

So Maisie has learned what the animals eat.
She knows that the Lion wants plenty of meat.
The monkeys like mangos, bananas and plums,
(She's also found out that they like pinching bums!).

The Parrot has fruit, or a handful of seeds
And lashings of veg. is what Elephant needs.

If penguins get fish then they'll give you a hug,
A meerkat is happy when chewing a bug.
Some bamboo for Panda and she's tickled pink,
The Camel likes hay and he might need a drink,

And Maisie gets hungry while she's having fun,
So Bertie has brought her a nice sticky bun!

We hope you've enjoyed Maisie's wonderful day,
Now, Bertie has something important to say;
"You may think that Maisie went round on her own,
But I was there watching - she wasn't alone.
Please don't feed the animals down at the zoo,
We zookeepers promise to do that for you."

PLEASE DO NOT FEED THE ANIMALS

Maisie and Bertie
support...

Help us to save Animals in the Wild

Animals in zoos are assured a good home,
But what of the ones who are destined to roam?
They live in the wild and face problems galore;
Their forests are taken and then, what is more,
They get into trouble for eating the crops
Of poor people who haven't got any shops.

Elephants in India and fierce tigers too
Need food to eat, just like the ones in the zoo.
World Land Trust buys land and then sets it aside
So they can roam freely and don't have to hide.
Reserves are protected by park guards and rangers
To make sure they're sheltered from all sorts of dangers.

Sir David Attenborough supports our Trust;
He thinks it's important and feels that we must
Save land for the animals while there's still time;
To lose them would be a most terrible crime.
While Bertie keeps animals safe in the zoo,
The future of wild ones rests with me and you.

By Viv Burton of the World Land Trust

WORLD LAND TRUST

The World Land Trust was established in 1989 to protect critically threatened habitats for their wildlife. So far over 500,000 acres have been saved throughout the world and are now protected by local organisations as nature reserves.

All donations resulting from the sale of this book will be used by World Land Trust's overseas project partners to fund park rangers who ensure that the reserves remain safe for animals in the wild.

World Land Trust is a registered charity No. 1001291. Its Patrons are Sir David Attenborough and David Gower.

A donation will save Real Acres in Real Places

For information or a School Pack please contact:
World Land Trust, Blyth House, Bridge Street,
Halesworth, Suffolk
IP19 8AB
Telephone: 01986 874 422

www.worldlandtrust.org

The End